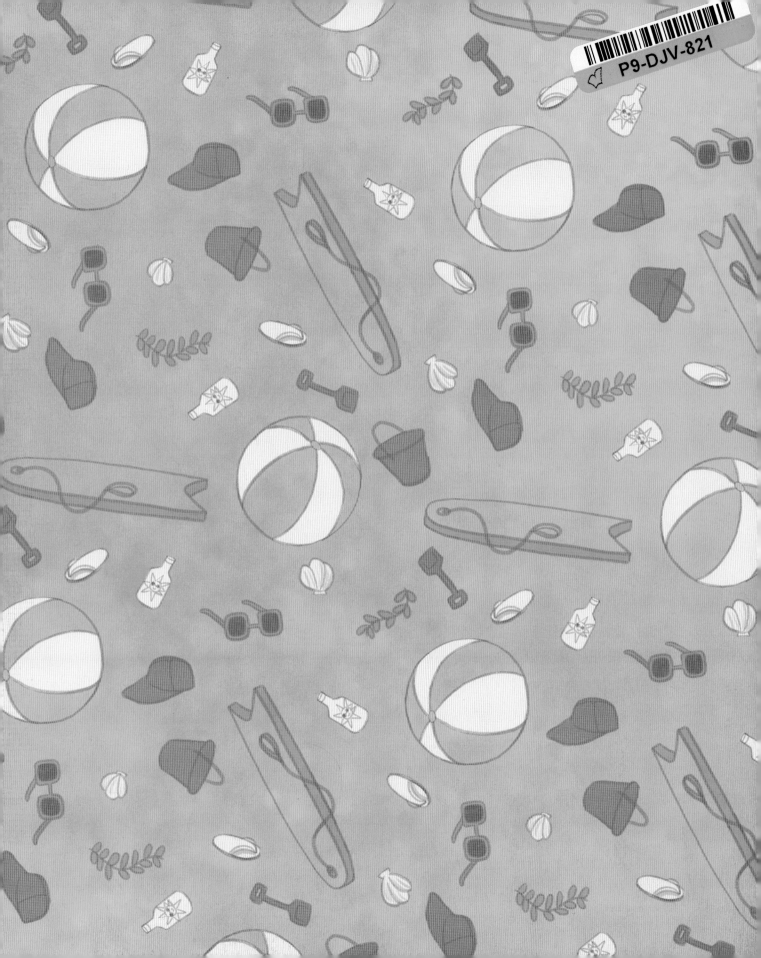

JULES VS. THE OCEAN

Jessie Sima

SIMON & SCHUSTER BOOKS FOR YOUNG READERS

New York London Toronto Sydney New Delhi

JULES is going to
make the BIGGEST . . .

FANCIEST . . .

MOST EXCELLENT castle
that has ever been built.

Her sister will be so impressed!

Maybe the Ocean will help!

Nope.

That's okay.

Jules will build an even bigger, fancier,
more excellent castle. All by herself.

Her sister will be
so impressed!

Jules thinks the Ocean might be out to get her.

Her sister assures her this happens to everyone.

If Jules wants to make the biggest, fanciest, most excellent castle, she will need to keep an eye on the Ocean.

Not today, Ocean.

Enough is enough.
Jules will NOT be pushed around.
She will stand her ground.

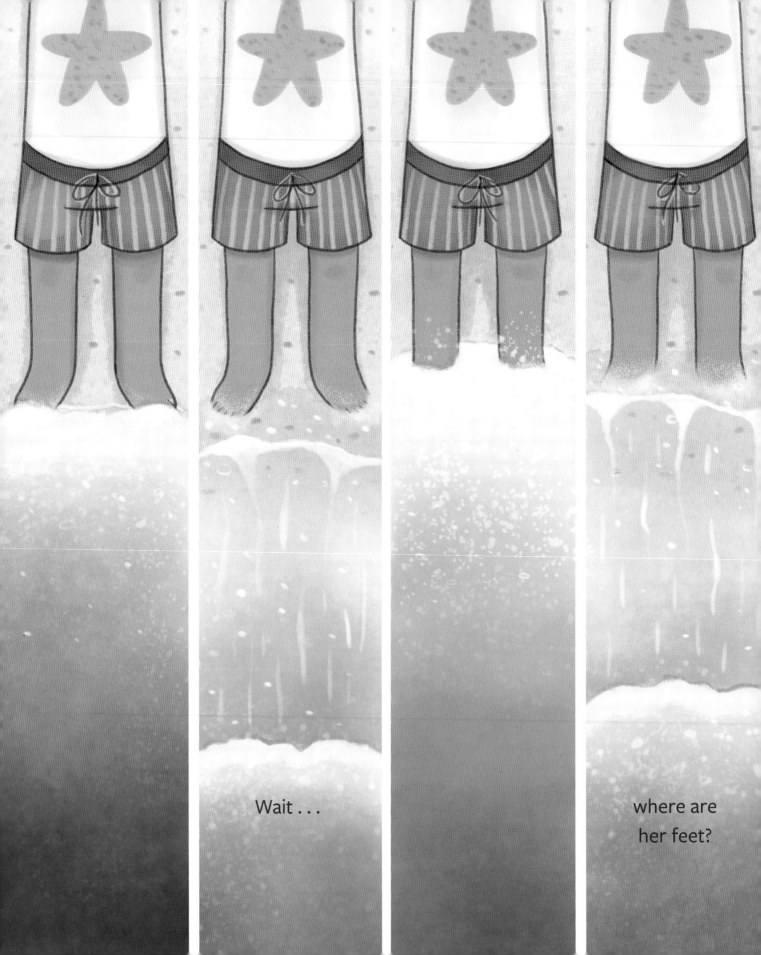

How is Jules supposed to build the biggest, fanciest, most excellent castle now?

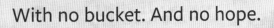

With no bucket. And no hope.

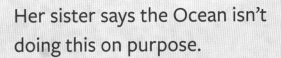

Her sister says the Ocean isn't
doing this on purpose.

Maybe she's right.

And who needs a bucket?

Jules cannot believe it!

Her sister is so impressed!

This is definitely the BIGGEST . . .

FANCIEST . . .

MOST EXCELLENT . . .

Uh-oh.

That was . . .

They tell their mom all about the castle,
and how the Ocean wanted to smash it!

Mom assures them that
happens to everyone.

Mom explains how the Ocean's waves
are controlled by lots of things. . . .

Mostly, the Moon.

Next time, Jules and her sister will
have to keep an eye on the Moon.

FOR DAD

SIMON & SCHUSTER BOOKS FOR YOUNG READERS

An imprint of Simon & Schuster Children's Publishing Division

1230 Avenue of the Americas, New York, New York 10020

Copyright © 2020 by Jessie Sima

All rights reserved, including the right of reproduction in whole or in part in any form.

SIMON & SCHUSTER BOOKS FOR YOUNG READERS is a trademark of Simon & Schuster, Inc.

For information about special discounts for bulk purchases, please contact Simon & Schuster Special Sales

at 1-866-506-1949 or business@simonandschuster.com.

The Simon & Schuster Speakers Bureau can bring authors to your live event. For more information

or to book an event, contact the Simon & Schuster Speakers Bureau at 1-866-248-3049 or visit our

website at www.simonspeakers.com.

Book design by Lizzy Bromley • The text for this book was set in Freight Sans.

The illustrations for this book were rendered in Photoshop.

Manufactured in China • 0220 SCP • First Edition

2 4 6 8 10 9 7 5 3 1

Library of Congress Cataloging-in-Publication Data

Names: Sima, Jessie, author, illustrator. • Title: Jules vs. the ocean / Jessie Sima.

Other titles: Jules versus the ocean

Description: First edition. | New York : Simon & Schuster Books for Young Readers, [2020] | Audience: Ages 4–8. |

Audience: Grades K–1. | Summary: Determined to build "the biggest, fanciest, most excellent sand castle" to impress her

sister, Jules is foiled again and again by the ocean.

Identifiers: LCCN 2019031377 (print) | LCCN 2019031378 (eBook) | ISBN 9781534441682 (hardcover) |

ISBN 9781534441699 (eBook)

Subjects: CYAC: Sand castles—Fiction. | Ocean—Fiction. | Beaches—Fiction | Sisters—Fiction.

Classification: LCC PZ7.1.S548 Jul 2020 (print) | LCC PZ7.1.S548 (eBook) | DDC [E]—dc23

LC record available at https://lccn.loc.gov/2019031377 | LC eBook record available at https://lccn.loc.gov/2019031378